WHY MONDAYS ARE AWESOME!

Sandra Knopp

Imprint

Bibliographic information from the German National Library: The German National Library lists this publication in the German National Bibliography; Detailed bibliographic data is available on the Internet at http://dnb.dnb.de.

Production and publishing: BoD – Books on Demand, Norderstedt

ISBN: 978-3-7583-0126-1

They're not.

They're not.

They're not.

They're not.

They're not.

They're not.

They're not.

They're not.

They're not.

They're not.

They're not.

They're not.

They're not.

They're not.

They're not.

They're not.

They're not.

They're not.

They're not.

They're not.

They're not.

They're not.

They're not.

They're not.

They're not.

They're not.

They're not.

They're not.

They're not.

They're not.

They're not.

They're not.

They're not.

They're not.

They're not.

They're not.

They're not.

They're not.

They're not.

They're not.

They're not.

They're not.

They're not.

They're not.

They're not.

They're not.

They're not.

They're not.

They're not.

They're not.

They're not.

They're not.

They're not.

They're not.

They're not.

They're not.

They're not.

They're not.

They're not.

They're not.

They're not.

They're not.

They're not.

They're not.

They're not.

They're not.

They're not.

They're not.

They're not.

They're not.

They're not.

They're not.

They're not.

They're not.

They're not.

They're not.

They're not.

They're not.

They're not.

They're not.

They're not.

They're not.

They're not.

They're not.

They're not.

They're not.

They're not.

They're not.

They're not.

They're not.

They're not.

They're not.

They're not.

They're not.

They're not.